HOW TO DATE AND OTHER TEENAGE FANTASIES

By
Ryan Michael Upton

Table of Contents

COPYRIGHT PAGE 5

CHAPTER 1 7

A Magical Night 7

CHAPTER 2 13

Ryan 13

CHAPTER 3 18

Cameron 18

CHAPTER 4 22

The Water Tower 22

CHAPTER 5 29

Wings 29

CHAPTER 6 37

Oceanside 37

CHAPTER 7 41

In the Sky 41

CHAPTER 8 46

The City 46

CHAPTER 9 48

The Alley 48

CHAPTER 10 55

Into the City 55

CHAPTER 11 58

Trouble in the Alley 58

CHAPTER 12 61

Steve 61

CHAPTER 13 64

Loopy Land 64

CHAPTER 14 73

The Maze 73

CHAPTER 15 79

The Man in the Hat 79

CHAPTER 16 88

Zebedee's Workshop 88

CHAPTER 17 91

The Maze Maker's Story 91

CHAPTER 18 94

Claire 94

CHAPTER 19 99

The Question 99

CHAPTER 20 102

The Girlfriend Factory 102

CHAPTER 21 105

Arrival at the Girlfriend Factory 105

CHAPTER 22 108

Inside the Factory 108

CHAPTER 23 111

Arrival at the Dance 111

CHAPTER 24 114
Social Chaos 114
CHAPTER 25 120
Emotional Turning Point 120
CHAPTER 26 137
Francis 137
CHAPTER 27 141
The Dance 141
CHAPTER 28 145
Bouncy Castle Party 145
CHAPTER 29 147
Leaving 147
CHAPTER 30 149
The After Party 149
CHAPTER 31 152
The Quiet Moment 152
CHAPTER 32 155
How to Date 155
CHAPTER 33 157
The Kiss 157
CHAPTER 34 160
Let's All Go to the Beach 160
CHAPTER 35 162
Sunrise 162

COPYRIGHT PAGE

HOW TO DATE AND OTHER TEENAGE FANTASIES

ISBN 978-1-7645764-4-4 (paperback)

First published in Australia in 2026.

Kindle Edition.

Cover design and illustrations by the author.

CHAPTER 1

A Magical Night

Mathew sat cross-legged on his bed, staring expectantly at the old man sitting beside the window.

"Alright," Mathew said. "Tell me one of your famous stories."

Uncle Ryan smiled faintly.

"I wasn't always this old, you know."

Mathew grinned.

"You're still pretty old."

Ryan laughed.

"That's fair."

He lifted his coffee mug carefully. His hands trembled slightly as he took a sip.

"These days," Ryan said, "my knees complain when I stand up too quickly. My hair's mostly grey. And the mirror shows a man I barely recognize."

Mathew tilted his head.

"You don't look that bad."

Ryan waved the compliment away.

"But once," he said, "a long time ago, I was young."

He looked toward the window for a moment.

"And the world felt enormous."

Mathew frowned thoughtfully.

"You? Young?"

Ryan's expression softened.

"When you're young," he said slowly, "every day feels like it might change your life."

He paused.

"But most days don't."

Mathew shrugged.

"Sounds boring."

Ryan chuckled.

"Most of them were."

He leaned back in the chair.

Ryan looked back at Mathew.

"But one night never did."

Mathew's eyes widened.

"What happened?"

Ryan smiled slowly, teasing.

"Even now, decades later, I remember it clearly."

Mathew sat quietly now.

Ryan continued.

"That time," he said, "I was just a teenager standing on the balcony of my parents' beach house."

"Looking out across the ocean, trying to figure out what to do with my life."

Mathew nodded slowly.

Ryan sighed.

Mathew blinked in disbelief. Dating?

Ryan nodded.

"Everyone else seemed to know the rules."

"But I felt like I'd missed the class where they explained everything."

Mathew laughed.

“That’s still happening.”

Ryan leaned forward slightly.

Ryan nodded.

“Because something happened that changed everything.”

Mathew raised an eyebrow.

“Aliens?”

Ryan shook his head calmly.

“Witches,” Ryan said calmly.

“Real ones.”

Mathew blinked.

“…what?”

Ryan grinned.

“Witches. Wizards. Warlocks.”

Mathew stared at him.

“That sounds fake.”

Ryan leaned back in his chair.

"At the time," he said, "I thought so too."

He glanced toward the window again.

"The evening was quiet."

"Cicadas buzzed in the trees."

"The sky turned orange as the sun dropped toward the ocean."

Ryan paused.

"Watching the road curve along the coastline."

Mathew interrupted.

"Let me guess."

Ryan smiled.

"A car."

Mathew nodded proudly.

Ryan pointed at him.

"Exactly."

"Headlights appeared around the bend."

The lights swept across the trees.

Ryan leaned forward slightly.

“And that…”

He paused.

“…was the moment everything began.”

Mathew shook his head slowly.

“I knew it.”

Ryan laughed.

CHAPTER 2

Ryan

Uncle Ryan studied Mathew for a moment.

“Before we go any further,” he said, “I should probably introduce myself properly.”

Mathew frowned.

“You’re Uncle Ryan.”

Ryan chuckled.

“Yes… Now I am.”

“But back then, I was a completely different person.”

Mathew tilted his head.

“How different?”

Mathew nodded immediately.

“Yeah, that sounds familiar.”

Ryan laughed.

“I wasn’t just lonely. I was terrified that everyone else understood life except me.”

“Everyone else seemed to know how dating worked.”

He shrugged.

"But mostly I was afraid of rejection."

Mathew leaned forward.

"So what did you do?"

Ryan folded his hands together.

"This story really did happen to me."

Ryan smiled faintly.

"Memory plays tricks on you."

"It softens the rough parts."

"And sometimes the most unbelievable moments begin to feel like dreams."

"The beach house, for example. It had a delicate, clean smell—like old summer days and sunburn cream."

Mathew smiled.

"My grandparents' place?"

Ryan nodded.

"It sat on a quiet stretch of coastline where the road curved beside the ocean."

"On one side, there was the sea."

"On the other side, there were houses tucked behind windswept trees."

Ryan looked thoughtful.

"In summer, the place was full of life."

"Families."

"Barbecues."

"Kids running along the beach."

"But that night…"

He paused.

"…the coast felt strangely quiet."

"I was standing on the balcony watching the road."

"Couples were walking along the beach. A girl wandered in the distance."

"Friends were laughing near the water."

"Everyone else seemed to be having a great time."

Ryan nodded.

Mathew squinted.

"So you just watched people?"

Ryan sighed.

"Pretty much. Sometimes, they watched me too."

Mathew laughed.

"That's a little creepy."

Ryan laughed too.

"Maybe a little."

Then his expression changed.

"But then something happened."

Mathew sat up straighter.

"The car?"

Ryan nodded.

"Yes."

"I had been standing there for several minutes when I finally heard it."

"An engine."

"At first it was faint, carried on the wind."

"Then the headlights appeared around the bend."

Ryan traced a slow curve through the air with his hand.

"The car moved along the road slowly."

"I expected it to keep driving."

"Most cars did."

"But this one didn't."

Mathew leaned forward.

"What did it do?"

Ryan smiled.

"It slowed down."

“Then it turned.”

Mathew’s eyes widened.

“Into the driveway?”

Ryan nodded.

“Yes.”

“The engine stopped.”

“And suddenly the whole world felt quiet again.”

Ryan opened his hands slowly.

“Then the car door opened.”

Mathew whispered, “Who was it?”

CHAPTER 3

Cameron

My name is Ryan.

And this story really happened to me.

Cameron immediately looked up toward the balcony.

"Ryan!" he shouted.

His voice carried easily through the evening air.

"Do you still have that goal of finding your forever girl?"

I laughed.

"Something like that!"

I headed down the stairs to meet him.

Cameron was already leaning casually against the car when I stepped outside, wearing the same confident grin he always seemed to have.

Cameron had wavy, shoulder-length black hair and dark sunglasses. He wore a bright blue shirt that appeared to shimmer, giving him a somewhat supernatural look. "Perfect," he said, clapping a hand on my shoulder.

"Tonight is going to be legendary."

Sometimes I wondered if Cameron knew things about the world that the rest of us didn't.

Looking back, I think that was why I liked being around him. I craved freedom. Cameron seemed to live inside it.

He studied art at the university, Fine Arts, something I barely understood. My world was mathematics and engineering.

Cameron's world was creativity, chaos, and possibility.

Where I saw systems and rules, Cameron saw doors waiting to be opened.

When you're young, that kind of energy is irresistible.

We sat together on the low wall beside the driveway while the wind rustled through the trees and the ocean waves rolled steadily against the shore below.

For a few minutes, neither of us spoke.

The night stretched around us, quiet, warm, and full of possibility.

Finally, Cameron broke the silence.

"You're thinking too small," he said.

I glanced at him.

"What?"

"If you want to impress girls," he continued, "you have to think bigger."

I laughed.

"Oh yeah? And how exactly do you do that?"

Cameron leaned back against the wall and looked up at the darkening sky.

"You know what tonight needs?"

"What?"

"Adventure."

I shook my head.

"That usually means trouble."

Cameron grinned.

"Sometimes. You know I have sisters, too."

He stood up and stretched.

"Come on," he said. "We're young. We're standing next to the ocean on a perfect night. We can't just sit around doing nothing."

I had to admit he had a point.

"So what's the plan?" I asked.

Cameron turned toward me slowly, the familiar mischievous smile spreading across his face.

"The water tower."

I groaned.

“Not that place.”

That was how most of Cameron’s plans began.

And almost none of them ended the way we expected.

Cameron laughed.

“You should be careful,” he said.

“One day I might jump off it.”

He said it jokingly, but something about the comment made my stomach tighten.

Cameron had always liked pushing things too far.

Testing limits.

Seeing how close he could get to the edge without falling.

At the time, though, it just felt like the beginning of another strange night.

So I climbed into the car.

The engine started.

A few minutes later, we were driving up the winding road toward the water tower above the town.

It would take years for me to understand that this was the moment everything changed.

CHAPTER 4

The Water Tower

The road curved upward through the hills until the tower appeared.

It rose out of the dark like something ancient and forgotten, a massive steel tank balanced on a single concrete spine, silhouetted against the fading sky. The last light of sunset burned behind it, turning the metal edges into sharp lines of gold and shadow.

Cameron pulled into the lookout and killed the engine.

Silence.

Not complete, never complete, but close.

Wind moved through the dry grass. Far below, waves struck the rocks with a steady, distant rhythm. The kind of sound you felt more than heard.

We stepped out of the car.

The air was cooler up here, salt and eucalyptus. The smell of the ocean carried all the way up the cliff.

For a moment, neither of us spoke.

Then Cameron walked toward the edge.

"Ryan," he said, almost casually, "have you ever noticed how small everything looks from up high?"

I followed, slower.

The view opened before us: the coastline stretching endlessly in both directions, the town scattered in soft lights below, the ocean reflecting the last orange streaks of the sun. A girl, in the distance, walked alone on the beach.

"It's a good view," I said.

Cameron smiled faintly.

"It's more than that."

He rested his hands on the railing.

"From up here… everything makes sense. Problems shrink. People shrink."

I glanced at him.

"That's one way to avoid dealing with them."

He laughed quietly.

"Or maybe it's the only honest way."

The wind picked up, tugging at his shirt.

He stepped away from the railing.

Toward the low concrete wall.

My stomach tightened.

"Cameron…."

He climbed up onto it like it was nothing.

Like the drop didn't exist.

Like the ocean hundreds of feet below wasn't waiting.

"Relax," he said, arms stretching out to his sides. "Perfect balance."

"That's exactly what people say before they…."

The wind shifted.

A sharp, sudden gust.

His foot slipped.

Just a fraction.

But it was enough.

"….fall."

Time slowed.

His body tilted forward.

Arms flailed not dramatically, not heroically, just instinct, raw and uncoordinated.

"Whoa…"

I moved without thinking.

"Cameron!"

My hand shot forward.

For a split second, a single, impossible second, I almost had him.

Fingertips brushed the fabric.

Then nothing.

Air.

He disappeared over the edge.

The world snapped back into motion.

The sound hit first.

A hollow rush of wind tore past the cliff.

Then silence again.

Too much silence.

I stumbled forward, heart hammering so hard it felt like it might break something inside my chest.

"No… no, no—"

I reached the edge and looked down.

The drop was endless.

Dark water smashed against jagged rocks far below, white spray bursting upward like broken glass.

But there was nobody.

No impact.

No movement.

Nothing.

My brain refused to process it.

He should have…

He should have…

"Ryaaaaan…"

The voice drifted upward.

Faint.

Distorted.

Impossible.

I froze.

Every muscle locked.

"…Cameron?"

No answer.

Just the wind.

Then—

"Down here."

I leaned forward slowly.

Carefully.

And saw it.

At first, just a shape.

A shadow against the cliff face.

Then it moved.

Rising.

Not climbing.

Not falling.

Rising.

My breath caught.

The figure lifted into the fading light.

And I saw him.

Calm.

Relaxed.

Hovering.

Like gravity had forgotten him.

My mind tried to reject it.

Rewrite it.

Force it into something that made sense.

It failed.

Completely.

"Not everyone," Cameron said, smiling slightly, "plays by the same rules."

Then the light shifted.

And I saw them.

Wings.

CHAPTER 5

Wings

Cameron didn't fall.

He let go.

For a moment, there was only empty air where he should have been.

Then—

He rose.

Not climbing. Not struggling. Rising.

Calmly. Effortlessly.

Like gravity had simply… stopped applying.

My breath caught in my throat.

"No…" I whispered.

He hovered just below the edge of the tower, the last light of the sun breaking across his silhouette.

Then something moved behind him.

At first, I didn't understand what I was seeing.

Then the shape unfolded.

Wings.

White. Vast. Alive.

Each feather caught the fading light, shifting as the wind moved through them, not resisting it, but working with it. Adjusting. Balancing. Holding him in place like it was the most natural thing in the world.

My mind rejected it instantly.

This isn't real.
This can't be real.

"Breathe," Cameron said.

I hadn't realized I'd stopped.

Air rushed back into my lungs, sharp and uneven.

"How…?" My voice cracked. "How are you doing that?"

He tilted slightly in the air, the wings correcting without effort.

"A different set of rules."

"That's not an answer."

He smiled faintly.

"It's the only one that matters."

The wind surged upward from the ocean, lifting him higher. The wings moved once, controlled, and he rose several meters as if the air itself wanted him there.

Effortless.

That was the worst part.

No strain. No drama.

Just… control.

“You fell,” I said. “I saw you fall.”

“Or,” he replied, “you saw me stop holding on.”

The words landed somewhere deep, but my brain couldn’t process them. Nothing made sense anymore.

The world had split open, and whatever was underneath didn’t follow any rules I understood.

Then the air changed.

The wind stilled.

The sound of the ocean dulled, like someone had turned down reality itself.

Cameron lifted his hands.

Slowly.

Deliberately.

Light threaded through the clouds above us, gold at first, soft and distant.

Then brighter.

Stronger.

Spreading.

The sky wasn't reflecting the sunset anymore.

It was generating something new.

"What are you doing?" I said.

He didn't answer.

The light bent.

Focused.

Turned.

Toward me.

Every instinct I had screamed to move.

I didn't.

It touched my hands.

Warm.

Not burning, just overwhelming.

Like stepping into sunlight after a lifetime in the dark.

It spread up my arms, through my chest, into everything.

My heart surged.

Faster. Harder.

Trying to keep up with something my body didn't understand.

"No, wait…"

The ground vanished.

Or I did.

For a split second, I thought I was falling.

That this was it…

Then the air caught me.

Not gently.

Firm. Unyielding.

Holding me exactly where I was.

I froze.

Afraid to move.

Afraid to breathe.

"I'm not…"

I looked down.

The tower.

The cliff.

The ocean.

All of it…

Below me.

I wasn't falling.

I was suspended.

“No…” I whispered.

Behind me…

Something shifted.

I turned, slowly.

Carefully.

And saw them.

Wings.

Mine.

They extended without effort, responding before I even understood how to control them. The wind moved through them, and they answered. Every adjustment translated instantly into balance.

Lift.

Stability.

Control.

Like my body had always known how to do this.

Like I’d just forgotten.

“Oh, my god…”

The words came out as a breath. Then a laugh.

Half disbelief.

Half something lighter.

Something free.

I moved, just slightly.

The wings caught the air.

And I rose.

A few meters. Effortless.

My heart was still racing.

The fear was still there.

But something else was stronger now.

For the first time….

I wasn’t stuck.

I wasn’t watching.

I wasn’t calculating every possible outcome.

I was in it.

Completely.

“I’m flying,” I said.

Cameron drifted closer, steady in the air.

“Technically,” he said, “you’re learning.”

I laughed.

I couldn’t stop.

The sky deepened around us, the last light of the sun fading into night. Below, the city flickered to life, thousands of lights turning on one by one.

A different world.

The one I thought I understood…

And the one opening in front of me.

Cameron turned, wings catching the wind.

"Ready?" he asked.

I hesitated.

Just for a second.

Then I looked out across the horizon.

At everything I thought I knew.

At everything I didn't.

"…Yeah."

And I leaned forward…

Into the sky.

CHAPTER 6

Oceanside

We landed harder than I expected.

My boots struck the metal platform with a hollow clang, the vibration running up through my legs and into my chest. For a moment, I just stood there, gripping the railing, trying to remember how gravity worked.

My heart was still racing.

A few seconds earlier, I had been suspended in open air, held up by something I didn't understand.

Now the world felt heavy again.

Solid.

Too solid.

"OK," I said, breathing unevenly. "I need an explanation."

Cameron touched down beside me like it was nothing, folding his wings with effortless precision. The feathers collapsed neatly behind his back and vanished into nothing, as if they had never existed.

"You handled that well," he said.

I stared at him.

"I grew wings."

He shrugged lightly.

"Minor adjustment."

I ran both hands through my hair, pacing once along the platform.

"Ten minutes ago, I was worried about dating."

I turned back to him.

"Now I'm flying over the ocean."

Cameron leaned casually against the railing, completely at ease.

"Perspective shift."

"That's not a perspective shift," I said. "That's a complete system failure."

He smiled faintly at that.

The wind moved around us, colder now, carrying salt from the ocean below. Far beneath the tower, waves crashed against the rocks in a steady, indifferent rhythm.

I looked out over the coastline.

Everything was still there.

The road. The houses. The beach.

Unchanged.

But I wasn't.

"It's not exactly the kind of thing you bring up casually."

I gave a short laugh.

"You could have tried."

Cameron pushed himself off the railing and stepped toward the edge again.

The height twisted something in my stomach.

"Cameron…"

He turned slightly, watching me.

I folded my arms.

"That was before you jumped off a cliff."

He smiled.

"And now?"

I looked past him.

At the drop.

At the open air.

At the impossible thing I had just done.

Fear was still there.

But something else sat beside it now.

Curiosity.

"…Now I want to understand it."

Cameron nodded once.

He stepped onto the edge.

The wind caught him immediately, pulling at his shirt.

I sighed.

"I had a feeling you were going to..."

CHAPTER 7

In the Sky

We climbed higher above the coastline, the wind rushing softly past.

For a moment, I forgot to be afraid.

The ocean stretched endlessly beneath us, glowing with the final orange light of the sunset. Waves rolled toward the beach in slow white lines, breaking gently against the shore.

From up here, everything looked different.

Smaller.

Simpler.

The winding coastal road curved along the cliffs like a silver ribbon. Tiny cars moved slowly along it, their headlights beginning to flicker on as evening settled across the town.

I laughed out loud.

"Wow," I said. "I can see everything."

Cameron floated easily beside me, barely needing to move his wings. A safe brother.

"Flying changes your perspective," he said.

"No kidding."

The water tower stood far below us now, casting a long shadow across the rooftops of the small seaside town. Houses that had once seemed large looked like toys scattered along the hills.

A sailboat drifted quietly across the ocean.

Even the waves looked calmer from this height.

I moved my wings cautiously, testing the motion again.

The air caught beneath and lifted me higher.

It felt strangely natural.

"You're getting the hang of it," Cameron said.

For a few minutes, we simply drifted above the coastline.

The wind carried the scent of salt and sea spray upward. The sky slowly deepened into shades of purple and blue as the sun slipped beneath the horizon.

Then Cameron pointed ahead.

Far in the distance, the city skyline shimmered against the darkening sky.

Tall buildings rose beside the water like glowing towers of glass.

Streetlights flickered on along a long bridge that stretched across the bay.

From this distance, the city looked alive.

Bright.

Endless.

“That’s where we’re going,” Cameron said.

I squinted toward the lights.

“You wanted adventure tonight.”

I smiled slightly.

Cameron followed my gaze.

“Your car,” I said.

Cameron grinned. He sensed my fear.

He shrugged.

Of course.

I shook my head slowly.

“Tonight is getting stranger by the minute.”

Cameron laughed.

“Just wait.”

We glided slowly.

Only a few hours earlier, I had been standing alone on a quiet balcony, worrying about how to talk to girls.

Now I was flying through the sky.

I looked over at Cameron.

We returned to the water tower.

The water tower approached quickly beneath us.

Cameron expertly drew a graceful curve to the top of the water tower, where he landed. My arc was less graceful.

We landed and made our way down the ladder to the car.

We drove the red car steadily toward the highway.

We made turns down roads leading towards the highway and the city.

Cameron nodded toward the skyline.

The city lights reflected across the dark water.

Suddenly, in the quiet confines of the car, I reflected on my flying experience. My world of rules, regulations, and work was gone. Replaced with a different world. A free world that was no longer crushed by obligations and responsibilities. A world where people were free to live in the gifts they were endowed with. A world where talent no longer had to hide, but rather was celebrated and enjoyed.

Cameron looked at me with a side eye, “You seem shaken, are you traveling OK?”

I nodded and suddenly thought of my parents. How could they possibly understand this new world I was now traveling in? Would they even want to? I thought of their pain, their fear. They would never be brave enough to release what kept them imprisoned. I suddenly felt completely alone. The feeling Cameron earlier described.

And for the first time in my life…

I wasn’t just watching the world.

I was soaring.

CHAPTER 8

The City

The coastline slowly faded behind us.

Ahead, the city rose from the water like a glowing island of glass and light.

Tall buildings stretched toward the sky, their windows reflecting the last colors of the sunset. Streetlights flickered on one by one, lining the long bridge that curved across the water.

Cars moved steadily along the road below, their headlights forming streams of white and gold.

The whole place looked alive.

Bright.

Endless.

The car drifted as we approached the bridge.

Our familiar red car drove along a road towards the city.

For a moment, I wondered how I had gotten here.

But then I realized something strange.

Flying had changed everything.

The world I had known only a few hours earlier suddenly felt far away, like it belonged to someone else.

The bridge stretched across the water like a ribbon of light leading straight into the heart of the city.

The skyline glowed ahead of us.

Music, laughter, and thousands of city lights waited beyond those towers.

Cameron glanced toward the buildings and smiled.

“This,” he said, “is where the real fun starts.”

The night had only just begun.

Somewhere, a tall girl spied on me.

And the city was waiting.

CHAPTER 9

The Alley

Mathew stared at Uncle Ryan.

"You expect me to believe," he said slowly, "that your best friend grew wings… and you just went along with it?"

Ryan smiled faintly.

"I didn't say I understood it."

Mathew folded his arms.

"That sounds fake."

Ryan chuckled.

"It did to me, too."

He leaned back slightly.

"But the strange part wasn't the flying."

Mathew frowned.

"What was?"

Ryan's expression shifted.

"The way everything after that… felt normal."

We parked behind a row of buildings just off the main street.

The engine cut.

Silence settled in.

Not the quiet of the ocean.

A different kind of quiet.

Closer.

Heavier.

The alley stretched ahead of us; narrow, enclosed, lit by a single flickering streetlight. Brick walls rose on either side, worn and uneven, carrying the faint smell of heat, dust, and something metallic.

Beyond the alley, the city breathed.

Distant music.

Laughter.

The low hum of traffic.

Life, just out of sight.

Cameron stepped out of the car first.

I followed.

The moment my feet hit the ground, something felt… off.

Not wrong.

Just unfamiliar.

Like stepping into a place that looked normal but wasn't.

Cameron didn't hesitate.

He walked toward the street as if he'd done this a hundred times before.

"Come on," he said.

"Welcome to the city."

I glanced back once.

The car sat where we left it.

Still.

Ordinary.

But for a brief second….

I turned away.

We moved deeper into the alley.

The light above us buzzed faintly, flickering just enough to make shadows shift at the edges of my vision.

I looked up.

Tall buildings boxed in the sky above, leaving only a narrow strip of deep purple night.

Everything felt closer here.

More intense.

More real.

A figure moved at the far end of the alley.

Then another.

People passing by.

Talking.

Laughing.

No one noticed us.

Or if they did…

They didn't care.

"That's it?" I said.

Cameron glanced back.

"What?"

"This is the city?"

He smiled slightly.

"You're expecting something different?"

I hesitated.

"…I don't know."

That wasn't true.

I had expected something bigger.

Louder.

More dramatic.

Instead…

It was just…

Life.

We stepped out onto the street.

And everything changed.

Light flooded in from every direction—storefronts, streetlamps, headlights reflecting off glass and pavement. Music spilled from open doorways. Voices overlapped, blending into a constant, living noise.

The city wasn't quiet.

It was alive.

I stopped for a moment.

Just taking it in.

People moved past us in every direction—laughing, arguing, talking, existing in ways that suddenly felt… effortless.

Like they understood something I didn't.

Cameron watched me.

"Overwhelming?" he asked.

I shook my head slowly.

"No."

I paused.

"…Just different."

He nodded once.

"Good."

We walked forward, merging into the flow of people.

And for the first time that night…

The sky.

The wings.

The impossible things I had just seen…

They didn't feel like the strangest part anymore.

Mathew leaned forward.

"So the city was normal?"

Ryan smiled.

"That's the trick."

Mathew frowned.

"What do you mean?"

Ryan looked toward the window.

"The world doesn't change all at once."

He paused.

"It changes just enough that you start to question what was normal in the first place."

Mathew sat quietly.

Thinking.

"…That's worse," he said.

Ryan laughed softly.

"Yeah," he said.

"It really is."

CHAPTER 10

Into the City

The city stretched ahead of us, long and quiet beneath the glow of yellow streetlights.

Behind us, the sound of the ocean had faded. Here, the air smelled different: warm brick, pavement, and the faint aroma of food drifting from restaurants somewhere beyond the buildings.

Cameron walked beside me, stealthily moving through the alley like he had been here a hundred times before.

I glanced up toward the skyline at the far end of the street.

The tallest buildings glowed against the deep purple sky, their windows shining like stars.

It was strange.

Only a short time ago, we had been standing on a quiet cliff by the ocean.

Now we were here, in the heart of the city, walking through narrow streets surrounded by towering buildings. Crowds of fellow young people, on busy missions of entertainment, eyed us down.

And somehow.

We had driven here.

Neither of us spoke for a moment.

Our footsteps echoed softly against the worn grey pavement as we moved farther down the alley.

A fire escape creaked slightly above us in the evening breeze.

Somewhere in the distance, a car horn sounded. Like someone trying to get attention but too shy to follow through.

Cameron finally broke the silence.

"So," he said casually, "what do you want to do first?"

I thought about it.

The city stretched endlessly around us, music, lights, people, and possibilities waiting in every direction.

I smiled.

"I don't know," I said.

"But tonight feels like something special."

Cameron nodded.

"Yeah," he said.

"I think you're right."

And together we walked deeper into the city night, ready to discover whatever the evening had planned for us.

CHAPTER 11

Trouble in the Alley

We had only walked a short distance down a connecting alley when two figures stepped out from the shadows.

They moved quickly.

Before we even had time to react, one of them grabbed Cameron by the collar and shoved him against the brick wall.

The other stepped in front of me.

Both of them had bright Mohawks that stood up like jagged flames, one red, one electric blue. Their jackets were covered with metal studs, and tattoos crawled across their arms.

Then I saw the knives.

The red-haired one pressed the blade close to Cameron's neck.

Cameron didn't move. He was relaxed, unafraid. A reaction I could not understand.

He stayed calm behind his dark sunglasses.

"What do you want?" Cameron asked.

The second man smirked and held his knife toward me.

"Your wallet."

My heart began pounding.

In the distance was the sound of a concerned girl screaming.

A few minutes earlier, we had been flying through the sky.

Now we were trapped in a narrow city alley with two armed strangers.

I slowly raised my hands.

"OK," I said cautiously.

"No problem."

But something about Cameron's expression didn't change.

He looked almost… bored. Like he knew they were joking.

Like this situation wasn't nearly as dangerous as it appeared.

The red-haired punk leaned closer.

"Don't make this difficult," he said, nervously, like he was having second thoughts.

The alley grew quiet.

The city lights flickered at the far end of the street.

And for a moment, everything seemed to pause.

Then Cameron smiled slightly. “A couple of hobgoblins in another form.”

And I suddenly had the feeling that these two had picked the wrong people to rob.

CHAPTER 12

Steve

The tension in the alley snapped like a pulled wire.

The punks were still holding their knives, the metal glinting under the streetlights, when a voice came from farther down the alley.

"Evening."

Everyone turned.

A tall blond-haired man stepped into the warm glow of the streetlamp. He wore a simple white tank top, his arms and neck covered in intricate tattoos that twisted like living artwork across his skin.

He walked toward us calmly, as if he had all the time in the world.

The two punks immediately stiffened.

The red-haired one glanced at the newcomer and lowered his knife slightly while calculating.

"Well," he muttered to his friend, "we'll be off then."

The blue-haired punk nodded quickly.

Neither of them seemed interested in continuing the confrontation anymore.

Without another word, they stepped back, slipping into the shadows of the alley as quickly as they had appeared.

Just like that.

They were gone.

I exhaled slowly, realizing I had been holding my breath.

Cameron looked toward the man who had just arrived and smiled.

“Ah,” Cameron said casually.

“It’s my friend Steve, um, he is also a magical person.”

Steve turned toward me.

“We might have been in trouble,” Cameron laughed.

Steve stopped a few steps away, hands relaxed at his sides.

“Looked like it, don’t believe everything Cameron says,” Steve said with a faint grin.

The city lights flickered behind him as the sounds of traffic and music drifted through the night air.

For a moment, the alley felt calm again.

Where Cameron was studious and calm, Steve appeared the opposite, boisterous and rebellious.

But I had the strange feeling that meeting Steve was about to make the night even more interesting.

CHAPTER 13

Loopy Land

The tension in the alley didn't end.

It thinned.

Like smoke.

We stood beneath a flickering streetlight, the city humming around us again as if nothing had happened. Cars passed somewhere beyond the buildings. Music drifted faintly through the night.

Normal.

Almost.

Steve leaned back against the brick wall, completely relaxed.

"Don't worry about those guys," he said. "They're mostly harmless. They work for me."

"Mostly."

I glanced at Cameron.

He didn't look concerned.

Which somehow made it worse.

"So," Cameron said, folding his arms, "where are you heading?"

Steve pushed himself off the wall.

"Loopy Land."

He said it like it meant something.

Like we should already understand.

"My girlfriend's there," he added. "Susan."

I frowned slightly.

Already, I felt behind.

Steve looked at both of us carefully.

"You can walk away now," he said.

"Most people do."

There it was again.

That choice.

That quiet moment where the night could still return to normal.

Go home.

Forget the wings.

Forget the alley.

Forget all of it.

I looked at Cameron.

He looked at me.

No words.

Just that same unspoken agreement we had since the water tower…

Keep going.

Cameron smiled.

"Sure," he said. "Why not?"

Steve turned and started walking.

"Come on," he called, already moving. "It's not far."

We followed.

Out of the alley.

Into the city.

The streets grew brighter as we moved.

More crowded. The ladies who followed, laughing.

More alive.

Laughter spilled from open doorways. Music pulsed through the walls. Neon reflections shimmered across windows and wet pavement.

The city wasn't quiet anymore.

It was awake.

Then….

It opened.

One moment, we were between buildings.

The next moment, we stepped into something else entirely. At first, it looked like a park.

Grass. Trees. Open space.

Then…

The paths moved.

Like changing relationships.

Not dramatically.

Not enough to draw attention.

Just… enough.

Lanterns glowed along winding walkways that curled through the grass like ribbons laid down by someone who didn't believe in straight lines.

Red.

Gold.

Blue.

Each path looping back on itself, crossing, bending, twisting into shapes that didn't quite settle.

Just like modern dating.

Colorful flags fluttered overhead.

Soft music drifted through the air.

And at the center….

A tower.

Cameron saw me staring and asked, “Are you married to that tower?”

It spiraled upward toward the sky, its structure folding in on itself in impossible geometry, like it had been designed without rules.

Or with different ones.

“This,” Steve said, turning back to us with a grin,

“is Loopy Land.”

I stared at it.

From here, the whole place felt wrong in a very specific way.

Not broken.

Not chaotic.

Deliberate.

“From above,” Cameron said quietly, “this would look like a maze.”

Steve smiled.

“It is a maze.”

I looked closer.

The wall curved, brightly colored, shifting almost imperceptibly.

A path that seemed open… wasn’t.

A turn that shouldn't exist… did.

Steve didn't answer immediately.

"My girlfriend should be somewhere inside," he added, scanning the paths.

"Unless the maze decided otherwise."

"The maze decides?" I said.

Steve glanced at me.

"You'll see."

And then…

She appeared.

Not walking toward us.

Not arriving from a distance.

Just…

There.

Susan stepped out from between two shifting paths as if she had always been part of them.

As if the maze had shaped itself around her.

She moved through the lantern light with effortless calm, her golden dress catching each flicker and turning it into something softer.

Warmer.

Intentional.

Steve smiled immediately.

"There she is."

I barely heard him.

Because something about her didn't feel accidental.

Susan didn't enter Loopy Land.

She belonged to it.

Behind her, the paths shifted again.

Quietly.

Almost politely.

I didn't answer.

I was watching the maze.

Because now that we were standing at the edge of it…

I could feel it.

Not physically.

Not exactly.

But in the same way, you feel someone looking at you from across a room.

Attention.

The paths curved.

Adjusted.

Opened.

Closed.

Reacting.

To us.

To me.

Steve gestured forward.

“Come on,” he said. “No point standing at the entrance all night.”

Susan watched us quietly.

Waiting.

Not impatient.

Not concerned.

Just… certain.

Like she already knew what we were going to do.

I hesitated.

Just for a second.

Because something deep in my chest tightened...

The same feeling I’d had on the balcony.

The same feeling before Cameron fell.

That sense that once you step forward…

Something changes.

Not outside.

Inside.

Cameron glanced at me.

"You coming?" he asked.

CHAPTER 14

The Maze

Up close, Loopy Land was even stranger than it looked from the outside.

The colorful walls curved and twisted in every direction, forming paths that looped around themselves like giant ribbons laid across the ground. Lanterns hung above the maze, casting warm circles of light that made the colors glow in the night.

For a while, we simply wandered.

Every corner revealed another turn.

Every turn led to another path.

"I have no idea where we are anymore," I said.

Behind me, Cameron stood on another winding path with his hands raised slightly, as he had just given up trying to understand the layout.

"Your guess is as good as mine," he replied.

The city skyline sparkled beyond the maze, and the spiral tower rose above the twisting paths like the center of some strange puzzle.

Steve said, "I am sure my girlfriend is somewhere in here. I was talking to her moments ago."

Cameron shrugged.

“Well,” he said, “this place is called Loopy Land.”

“I guess getting lost is part of the experience.”

I turned another corner, following a path that curved gently toward the spiral tower.

For a moment, the maze seemed completely silent.

Loopy Land was bigger on the inside.

From the entrance, it had looked simple.

Inside…

It wasn’t meant to be solved.

The walls curved in bright ribbons; red, yellow, blue, looping just enough to feel familiar, never enough to feel certain. Lanterns glowed overhead, steady and watchful.

Too steady.

Steve stopped at an intersection and turned slowly.

“…this isn’t right.”

Every path looked almost the same.

Close enough to confuse. A type of modern dating.

Different enough to mislead.

“Guys?” he called.

No echo.

No answer.

A few turns away, Cameron frowned at the path behind us.

“We didn’t come from there.”

“Yes, we did,” I said.

Then paused.

The wall had shifted.

Not enough to see…

Just enough to doubt.

“… OK,” Cameron said quietly.

“The maze is moving.”

It wasn’t.

It just hadn’t decided what it was yet.

Deeper inside, Steve found Susan standing beneath a lantern, calm and still.

“There you are,” he said.

“Took you long enough,” she replied.

“…This place changed,” he said.

Susan smiled faintly.

“Of course it does.”

Back in the maze, we stopped at another intersection.

Four paths.

All wrong.

"New plan," I said, pointing upward.

"We head for the tower."

Cameron looked at it.

"…The one that hasn't gotten any closer?"

"…Yes."

We walked.

The path curved.

Looped.

Returned.

The tower stayed in front of us.

Never closer.

Behind us, the path shifted.

Quietly.

Gone.

I stopped.

"…Did you hear that?"

"Nothing," Cameron said.

Exactly.

The maze didn't move loudly.

It changed in silence.

Ahead…

Laughter.

Faint.

Familiar.

We turned toward it.

The path opened.

Deliberately.

For a moment…

Everything aligned.

The maze made sense.

The tower felt closer.

Then…

The lantern flickered.

The path split.

Three directions.

Where there had been one.

Cameron exhaled.

"…I hate this place."

I stared at the shifting walls.

At the impossible turns.

In the way every choice felt important…

even when it wasn't.

And I understood something.

This wasn't just a maze.

It wasn't trying to trap us.

It was trying to confuse us.

Test us.

Mirror us.

Above, the spiral tower turned slowly against the night sky.

Waiting.

And somewhere inside Loopy Land…

The maze kept changing.

Not randomly.

Deliberately.

Like it was learning us.

CHAPTER 15

The Man in the Hat

The maze didn't feel random anymore.

That was the problem.

It *looked* random, bright walls, looping paths, lanterns swaying gently overhead, but the longer we walked, the more it felt like something was… adjusting.

Watching.

We turned another corner.

The path split.

Then shifted.

Not dramatically.

Just enough.

"… OK," Cameron said quietly. "That's not normal."

I didn't answer.

Because I was watching the wall behind us.

It had moved.

Not while we were looking.

That was the unsettling part.

The maze didn't change in front of you.

It changed when you *weren't paying attention.*

Ahead, the spiral tower stood above everything, unchanged, unreachable.

Still distant.

Still watching.

"New plan," I said.

Cameron glanced at me.

"If you say 'head for the tower' again…"

"We follow something that *doesn't move.*"

He paused.

"…Like what?"

I didn't answer.

Because something else had entered the maze.

Not a sound.

Not movement.

Presence.

The kind you feel before you understand why.

Cameron stiffened slightly.

"…You feel that?"

I nodded.

We weren’t alone anymore.

At the far end of the path…

Someone stood.

Perfectly still.

Dressed in black.

Long coat.

Tall hat.

For a moment, I thought he hadn’t been there before.

Then I realized…

He had.

We just hadn’t noticed.

Cameron narrowed his eyes.

“…Was he there a second ago?”

“I don’t think that’s the right question.”

The man stepped forward.

Slow.

Measured.

The lantern light caught the edges of his coat, revealing fine brass buttons running down the front. A pair of goggles rested above the brim of his hat, glinting softly.

Out of place.

And yet…

More fitting than anything else in the maze.

He stopped a few meters away.

Smiled.

Not wide.

Not friendly.

Certain.

"You look lost," he said.

Cameron folded his arms.

"Understatement."

The man tilted his head slightly, as if considering that.

"Yes," he said calmly. "That tends to happen here."

I studied him.

"You've been watching us."

It wasn't a question.

He didn't deny it.

"I prefer to observe before I introduce myself."

The man smiled slightly wider.

Then, with a small, almost theatrical gesture, he tipped his hat.

“My name is Zebedee.”

The name hung in the air.

Like it mattered.

I gestured around us.

“You built this place.”

Again—not a question.

Zebedee’s eyes flicked briefly toward the shifting walls.

Then back to me.

“Built is a strong word,” he said.

“I guide it.”

As if on cue…

A section of wall behind him slid sideways.

Silent.

Effortless.

Revealing a path that hadn’t existed a moment ago.

Cameron took a step back.

“… OK.”

Zebedee didn’t turn.

Didn't react.

Like the maze was simply… continuing a conversation with him.

"The maze responds," he said calmly.

"To hesitation. To certainty. To people who think they understand it."

I frowned.

"And what does it do to people who don't?"

Zebedee's smile sharpened slightly.

"It shows them something interesting."

A pause.

Then…

"It showed me you."

The words landed heavier than they should have.

Cameron exhaled slowly.

"…That's not reassuring."

Zebedee ignored him.

His attention stayed on me.

Measured.

Deliberate.

"You're not following the pattern," he said.

I blinked.

"What pattern?"

He gestured vaguely toward the maze.

"Most people enter looking for something simple."

"Fun. Distraction. Someone else."

He stepped closer.

"But you…"

A slight pause.

"…you're asking the wrong questions."

I crossed my arms.

"Or the right ones."

For the first time…

Zebedee seemed genuinely interested.

A flicker.

Small.

But real.

"Yes," he said quietly.

"…possibly."

Behind us, the maze shifted again.

A path is closed.

Another opened.

The tower remained exactly where it had always been.

Unreachable.

Zebedee turned slightly, gesturing toward a narrow path that curved away from the maze's center.

"Come with me," he said.

Cameron didn't move.

"Why?"

Zebedee glanced back.

"Because wandering will take you in circles."

A beat.

"And I don't think you came here to stay lost."

Silence.

The maze hummed quietly around us.

Waiting.

Watching.

Cameron looked at me.

This time, there was no joke.

No sarcasm.

Just the same question we'd been answering all night.

Keep going?

I looked back at Zebedee.

At the path that hadn't existed before.

At the maze that was no longer pretending to be random.

Then I nodded.

"…Alright."

Zebedee smiled.

Not warmly.

But approvingly.

"Good," he said.

And for the first time…

The maze stopped resisting us.

CHAPTER 16

Zebedee's Workshop

The maze slowly faded behind them as Zebedee led the group through a quiet side gate of Loopy Land.

Beyond the carnival lights, the city stretched upward in towers of glass and steel. Cars moved like glowing ants along the streets below.

I tilted my head back.

"Wait… we're leaving the park?"

Zebedee smiled slightly.

"Only for a moment."

They walked several blocks through the calm night streets until they reached a tall apartment building standing above the city.

Lights glowed in scattered windows, but in one apartment on the top floor, one shone brighter than all the others.

Warm golden light spilled from enormous windows.

Inside, strange shapes could be seen moving.

Gears.

Machines.

Spinning brass wheels.

Cameron pointed upward.

“Is that… your place?”

Zebedee followed his gaze.

“Yes.”

I squinted.

“It looks like a laboratory.”

“Workshop,” Zebedee corrected.

They stepped inside the building and rode the elevator silently upward.

When the doors opened, warm mechanical sounds filled the hallway.

Tick.

Whirr.

Click.

Zebedee unlocked the door.

The moment it opened, my eyes widened.

The entire apartment was filled with strange mechanical inventions.

Clockwork devices spun slowly on worktables.

Brass gears rotated inside glass chambers.

Maps of the maze hung across the walls, filled with notes and strange symbols.

Cameron walked forward carefully.

“You built all this?”

Zebedee stepped inside calmly.

I looked back toward the glowing city skyline outside the windows.

Zebedee smiled quietly.

“Loopy Land requires constant… adjustment.”

I stared at one of the blueprints.

It looked like a diagram of the maze.

But the paths were **moving**.

Sliding.

Shifting.

I slowly looked up.

“You’re the one moving the maze.”

Zebedee folded his hands behind his back.

“Someone has to keep it interesting.”

Behind them, the city lights shimmered beneath the quiet crescent moon.

CHAPTER 17

The Maze Maker's Story

The warm light of Zebedee's workshop filled the room with a soft golden glow.

I sank deeper into the leather chair, holding a cold bottle in my hand while trying to take in everything around me.

The walls were covered in gears, pipes, and spinning clockwork mechanisms. Dozens of old clocks ticked quietly in different rhythms.

Tick.
Tick.
Tick.

Cameron leaned forward, studying a massive brass mechanism turning slowly near the ceiling.

"You built all of this?"

Zebedee sat comfortably in the center chair, swirling the drink in his glass.

Steve stretched out on the couch beside his girlfriend, completely relaxed.

I looked from the machinery to Zebedee.

Cameron raised his bottle.

"You invite lost people to your apartment?"

Zebedee smiled.

I raised an eyebrow.

Zebedee leaned forward slightly.

“Most people visit Loopy Land to have fun.”

He gestured toward the glowing maze outside.

I glanced sideways at Cameron.

Cameron shrugged.

Steve laughed quietly.

“That’s actually pretty accurate.”

I looked back at Zebedee.

“So what exactly are we searching for?”

Zebedee took a slow sip from his glass.

Then he set it down on the table.

I frowned.

Zebedee nodded slowly.

Cameron tilted his head.

Zebedee smiled again.

But this time the smile carried a hint of mystery.

“That,” he said calmly,

“is the part everyone has to discover for themselves.”

Outside the window, far below the apartment tower, the colorful paths of **Loopy Land** twisted quietly under the moonlight.

CHAPTER 18

Claire

The warm glow of the workshop lamps reflected off the brass gears and polished pipes that lined the walls.

I sat quietly, trying to absorb everything I had seen that night.

The moving maze.
The strange park.
Zebedee's impossible machines.

At that moment, the door to the workshop opened.

Everyone turned.

Two women approached the doorway. The first stepped inside, while a second—tall and slender—hesitated just out of view. I caught a flash of long hair, a shyness, then the woman behind was gone in fear of discovery. The first woman remained blocking the doorway, giving the appearance that she was protecting a secret and hiding the second woman from view.

Her short bright blue hair caught the warm light of the hanging lamps. She wore a brown leather outfit decorated with small brass buckles and gears, almost like something built for exploring strange mechanical worlds.

I blinked.

"Well… that's new."

Zebedee smiled.

"Perfect timing."

The woman walked calmly across the room and dropped into the empty chair beside me.

"Sorry, I'm late," she said casually.

Cameron looked from her to Zebedee.

"You invited more people?"

Zebedee nodded.

I asked, "And you are?"

The woman grinned.

Across the room, Zebedee leaned comfortably back in his tall leather chair, one hand resting on the armrest while the other held a small glass.

He looked toward the couple sitting beside him.

"Let me introduce you to my girlfriend, Claire."

Cameron and I both turned our heads.

Claire smiled warmly.

Up close, I could see that she seemed completely at ease in the strange mechanical apartment.

Susan leaned slightly into Steve, her golden dress catching the soft glow of the lamps.

Cameron nodded politely.

“Nice to meet you.”

Claire lifted her glass.

I glanced between Claire and Zebedee.

“So… you two met in the maze?”

Steve chuckled.

“Something like that.”

Zebedee leaned forward slightly.

“Loopy Land has a habit of bringing interesting people together.”

I thought of the girl who had disappeared, out of sight, when Claire walked in.

Gears rotated slowly inside glass cases.

The huge window behind Zebedee framed the glowing city skyline beneath the moon.

Cameron took a sip from his bottle.

Zebedee smiled.

“Now…”

He pointed toward a large mechanical model sitting on the worktable beside him.

It was a miniature version of the entire maze.

But unlike the real maze…

This one was **moving**.

Tiny walls slid slowly through the model.

Paths appeared.

Others disappeared.

I leaned forward.

I stared at the shifting miniature paths.

Zebedee's smile widened slightly.

The workshop felt warmer now.

More alive.

The lamps glowed softly against the brass gears and copper pipes that covered every wall. The slow ticking of clocks blended with the quiet hum of the machines.

I leaned back in my chair, starting to relax.

For the first time since entering Loopy Land, the night felt almost normal.

Almost.

Across the room, Zebedee sat calmly in his tall leather chair, glass in hand, watching the group with quiet amusement.

Steve's girlfriend, Susan, rested comfortably beside Steve, smiling as she listened to Cameron explain how badly he had gotten lost in the maze.

Zebedee raised his glass slightly.

"The maze enjoys confusing people."

Claire reached over and grabbed one of the bottles from the table.

"Explorer," she added.

I looked around the room again.

The strange machines.

The maze keeper.

The mysterious couple.

And now… an explorer.

He slowly nodded.

"OK," I said.

Zebedee leaned back in his chair, clearly enjoying the moment.

"Oh, Ryan," he said.

CHAPTER 19

The Question

Claire leaned back comfortably in the leather chair, crossing one boot over the other as she looked around the room.

Outside the tall windows, the city shimmered beneath the moonlight.

She took a slow sip from the bottle she had grabbed from the table.

Then she smiled.

"What are all you guys up to tonight?"

I shrugged.

Claire glanced toward Zebedee.

"You brought them here?"

Zebedee nodded calmly.

"They seemed curious."

Claire tilted her head, studying Cameron and me more carefully.

"Curious people usually end up in interesting situations."

Zebedee rested his hand on the edge of the table.

The room grew quiet.

The ticking clocks seemed louder now.

Zebedee smiled faintly.

Zebedee looked toward the glowing maze outside the window.

Claire looked at Zebedee and asked, “What are you guys up to tonight?”

Claire’s words hung in the warm air of the workshop.

“I’m trying to find a girlfriend,” I blurted out, then, with no way to claw the words back in, I sat slightly embarrassed.

For a moment, nobody spoke, increasing my embarrassment.

Then Cameron burst out laughing.

“Of all the mysterious things to say in a room full of clockwork machines…”

Steve chuckled too, lifting his bottle.

“Honestly? That might be the most normal thing said tonight.”

Susan smiled softly from beside him, resting her head against Steve’s shoulder.

Across the room, Claire leaned forward in her chair, her bright blue hair catching the golden light of the hanging lamps.

She studied me for a moment.

“You came to the maze looking for someone?”

I shrugged, “Maybe someone was looking for me?”

Zebedee swirled the drink in his glass thoughtfully.

“The maze has a curious habit,” he said slowly.

I looked up.

“What habit?”

Zebedee smiled faintly.

“It tends to show people what they’re looking for.”

Cameron frowned.

“That sounds suspiciously like a fortune cookie.”

Claire laughed.

“No, he’s serious.”

She leaned forward and tapped the table, where the miniature maze slowly shifted and changed. A small black figure appeared to creep across the miniature maze, and then was gone.

“The maze responds to people.”

Claire tilted her head.

CHAPTER 20

The Girlfriend Factory

Zebedee smiled calmly, as if he had just suggested getting pizza.

“A girlfriend? That’s easy, just go to the Girlfriend Factory. Come on, I’ll take you.”

I blinked.

“A… what?”

Across the room, Cameron lowered his bottle slowly.

“Did you just say **Girlfriend Factory**?”

Zebedee smiled calmly.

“Yes.”

I leaned forward in my chair.

“That sounds extremely illegal.”

Claire burst out laughing.

“It’s not a factory like that.”

Susan covered her mouth, trying not to laugh as Steve shook his head.

“You should see Ryan’s face right now.”

I pointed at Zebedee.

"You just told me to go to a factory to get a girlfriend. I feel like I'm missing several steps of logic."

Zebedee stood slowly from his chair and walked toward the large window overlooking the city.

He gestured.

"The Girlfriend Factory is a deeper attraction, where people magically, apart from this world, meet and even date."

Cameron frowned.

"People enchanted with magical gifts?"

Claire leaned forward.

"Parts of this world most visitors never find."

I crossed my arms.

"And somehow you expect me to believe there's a place, this magical place that... manufactures girlfriends?"

Zebedee chuckled.

"No."

He turned back toward them.

"It **introduces** people. Magical people."

I raised an eyebrow.

"Introduces people?"

Zebedee nodded.

“To the person they’re meant to meet. Their destined ones. Good or Bad.”

The room grew quiet again.

Even the ticking clocks seemed to pause for a moment.

I looked around the room at everyone sitting comfortably in the strange mechanical workshop.

Then he pointed toward the window.

He paused.

I asked, “There’s a place that helps people find each other?”

Claire smiled.

“That’s one way to describe it, fated, soul partners.”

I slowly stood up.

“Well then,” he said.

“Let’s go find this factory.”

CHAPTER 21

Arrival at the Girlfriend Factory

The group stepped out of Zebedee's building and followed him through the glowing night streets.

The city buzzed with energy.

Neon reflections shimmered across the river. Music echoed faintly from somewhere in the distance. I had expected a quiet little building hidden somewhere.

Instead.

They arrived at something enormous.

I stopped walking.

"OK… that's definitely a factory."

Before them stood a massive industrial complex glowing with warm golden light, tall smokestacks stretched toward the sky like giant chimneys, their tops glowing softly as steam drifted into the night.

A large circular stained-glass window rested in the center of the building.

Across the front of the building, bright letters read:

FACTORY

Colored laser lights shot into the sky above it, sweeping slowly across the clouds like a giant celebration.

And in front of the entrance.

A long line of people, zombies, warlocks, goblins, and witches waited behind velvet ropes. I recognized the hobgoblin punks from before, waiting in line.

Cameron blinked.

"That's a lot."

I looked closer.

The strange crowd stretched halfway down the street.

Steve laughed quietly.

"Told you it was popular."

Susan squeezed Steve's arm.

Steve nodded.

"Worth it."

I stared at the massive glowing building.

Claire explained.

"They're hoping to meet someone, someone magical, and someone with certain gifts."

I responded, "This might be the strangest dating system I've ever seen."

Zebedee stepped forward toward the front gate.

The guards appeared to recognize Zebedee and immediately opened the velvet rope for him.

The crowd murmured, with frustrated jealousy, as we passed.

I leaned toward Cameron.

"Does he own this place, too?"

Cameron whispered back.

"At this point, I wouldn't be surprised."

Zebedee looked back over his shoulder and smiled.

"Well then," he said.

"Let's see if the factory has someone waiting for you."

CHAPTER 22

Inside the Factory

The moment they stepped through the giant factory doors, I froze.

A wall of music confronted us.

This was not what I expected.

Not machines.

Not conveyor belts.

Not rows of robotic arms assembling girlfriends.

Instead…

It was a party.

A massive hall stretched out before them, glowing with golden light. Colored laser beams cut through the air while a giant disco ball spun slowly above the crowd.

Music thundered through the room.

Hundreds of people danced across the floor while a group of DJs worked behind a glowing booth at the far end of the hall.

Cameron stared in disbelief.

Steve laughed over the music.

"Yep."

I looked around.

Susan leaned close to Steve.

"It's like a meeting place."

Claire turned around and walked backwards through the crowd, smiling at me.

"Be very careful you don't get into trouble with the nasty types."

I frowned.

"Nasty types?"

Claire gestured toward the dancing crowd around them.

"The Serpents, Mephistopheles."

I slowly nodded.

"So the Girlfriend Factory…"

Cameron, pretending to be ignorant, finished the thought:

"…is basically the world's most complicated matchmaking system for people with a bit of magic inside them."

Zebedee appeared beside them again, completely calm despite the roaring music.

"Exactly."

I watched the crowd dancing beneath the spinning lights.

Some people were talking.

Some were laughing.

Some were being eaten.

Some were already holding hands.

I scratched the back of my head again.

“So I guess this place doesn’t actually give you a girlfriend.”

Zebedee smiled.

“No.”

He gestured toward the crowded dance floor.

“It simply brings you to the right room.”

CHAPTER 23

Arrival at the Dance

I barely had time to react before he was pulled into the crowd.

Music pounded through the giant hall while the disco ball scattered glittering light across hundreds of moving bodies.

Claire grabbed his hand and pulled him toward the center of the dance floor.

"Relax!" she shouted over the music.

"This is the easy part!"

I looked around nervously.

"I thought this place was about finding girlfriends!"

Claire laughed.

"It is!"

Then she pointed toward the center of the circle forming around them.

"Step one…"

Cameron suddenly appeared beside me, grinning.

"…you survive the dance floor."

Susan clapped as Steve raised his hands and cheered with the crowd.

People began forming a circle around the group as the music shifted into a heavier beat.

I looked at Cameron.

Cameron shrugged.

“Maybe they’re judging our dancing.”

I sighed.

Claire smiled mischievously, “Get ready to perform the incantation spell.”

I stared at her, confused.

I rubbed my face.

Cameron patted him on the shoulder.

“Well? Do you know how to dance?”

I stood in the middle of the dance floor, the lights spinning across the room like colorful lightning. The crowd surrounded them in a huge circle. The rhythmic music was intoxicating.

He glanced nervously at Cameron. All eyes were on them.

Cameron grinned. He raised his hands, and a magical aura started to descend.

Before Cameron could answer, Zebedee stepped forward confidently, adjusting his hat under the flashing lights. Magic appeared to stream from Zebedee. They started to form a ring, surrounded by magical fire.

Zebedee danced majestically in rhythm to the music. Zebedee smiled and said, "Welcome to the **Girlfriend Factory!**"

The crowd roared with excitement.

CHAPTER 24

Social Chaos

Susan stepped beside Claire, smiling mischievously. They joined the ring, chanting the incantations.

Claire leaned toward me.

"Don't worry," she said. "It's mostly harmless."

I frowned.

"Mostly?"

On the stage, the DJ lowered the music slightly.

"The rules are simple!" Zebedee continued. He pointed toward me.

I rubbed the back of my neck.

"This suddenly feels like a terrible idea."

Susan laughed.

"Relax," she said. "It's just a game."

Cameron folded his arms.

"Yeah," he added. "What's the worst that could happen?"

The lights dimmed.

The disco ball began to spin faster.

The music exploded back to life.

I sighed.

“I should have stayed home tonight.”

Zebedee tilted his head slightly and gestured toward the grand staircase rising behind him.

A portal to another world appeared to open. I squinted in disbelief.

Golden light spilled down the steps, and the crowd instinctively turned to look.

I followed Zebedee’s gaze.

“The girlfriends walk down that staircase.”

I blinked. Dead girlfriends? Risen from the grave?

“That sounds… very theatrical.”

Zebedee smiled faintly.

Claire leaned closer to Susan and whispered, “This is my favorite part.”

Susan grinned.

From the DJ booth, the music slowly faded into a dramatic orchestral build.

The massive stained-glass doors at the top of the staircase began to glow with an unnatural feel.

The crowd hushed.

Someone near me whispered, “Here it comes.”

I swallowed nervously.

“Here what comes?”

Zebedee adjusted his goggles.

The doors at the top of the staircase slowly creaked open.

Light flooded into the hall.

Silhouettes appeared at the top of the stairs.

The crowd gasped.

Cameron nodded.

He pointed toward the staircase.

The crowd fell completely silent.

From the glowing doorway at the top of the staircase, a single figure stepped forward.

A woman in flowing black descended slowly, almost floating. Her dark gown trailed behind her like drifting smoke. The golden light from the stained-glass window framed her silhouette, giving her an almost supernatural presence.

Every step echoed through the hall.

I leaned toward Cameron and whispered, “She doesn’t look like she belongs in a *Girlfriend Factory*, and she looks like she doesn’t belong to this world!”

Cameron nodded slowly.

"No… she looks like she owns the place."

Susan folded her arms, watching carefully.

Claire tilted her head.

"Well," she said quietly, "this just got interesting."

Zebedee smiled faintly, clearly enjoying the moment.

The mysterious woman stopped halfway down the staircase and looked out over the crowd.

Her eyes moved across the room… until they stopped.

Directly on me.

The music faded to a low, dramatic hum.

I shifted nervously, afraid.

"Why is she looking at me?"

Zebedee chuckled softly, "Tonight, you are the chosen one."

"Because," he said, adjusting his hat, "the factory always notices its newest member."

The woman began ghostly gliding down the final steps.

And the crowd slowly parted, making a path for her.

I leaned closer to Cameron, his voice low.

“Please tell me this is normal.”

Cameron watched the mysterious woman descending the staircase, clearly fascinated.

“No,” he said calmly. “This is definitely not normal.”

I glanced sideways at Zebedee.

“You knew about this, didn’t you?”

Zebedee didn’t answer immediately. Instead, he watched the woman approach with an expression that was somewhere between curiosity and amusement.

“Let’s just say,” Zebedee finally replied, “the factory occasionally likes to make a dramatic entrance.”

I frowned.

Cameron nodded toward the staircase.

“Look.”

The woman had nearly reached the bottom step. The crowd had parted completely now, forming a clear path through the hall.

The music had faded to a quiet, ominous rhythm.

I shifted uneasily. “Is she going to haunt me?”

Cameron shrugged slightly.

“Because,” he said, “nobody knows what exactly is going to happen.”

I blinked.

"I am being picked, me?"

Zebedee adjusted his hat and smiled.

"You."

I froze.

"…What?"

The woman stepped off the final step.

And began walking directly toward me.

CHAPTER 25

Emotional Turning Point

I stepped backward, raising my hand.

"No."

The word echoed louder than expected.

The crowd gasped.

Music in the hall stuttered to a halt.

The mysterious woman in black stopped only a few steps away, her dark eyes fixed calmly on me. The long shadows of her flowing gown drifted across the floor like smoke.

Cameron whispered under his breath, afraid.

"Did you just say no?"

I swallowed.

"Yes."

Cameron said, "Glad I'm not you."

Zebedee slowly turned toward me, clearly amused, "Don't upset her now."

"Ryan," he said softly, "people usually wait until after the selection to refuse."

I shook my head.

"I didn't come here to be… selected."

The woman tilted her head slightly, studying me with quiet curiosity.

Around them, the crowd began murmuring.

Susan leaned toward Claire.

"Well," she said with a grin, "that's new."

Claire nodded.

"Very new."

The mysterious woman took one more step forward.

Her voice, when she spoke, was calm and strangely gentle.

"Interesting."

I stiffened.

"Most people," she continued, "run."

She looked directly into my eyes.

"You're the first one who tried to walk away."

The room fell silent again.

Zebedee smiled slowly, "That's trouble."

"Oh," he said quietly, "He is with friends."

"Now the night just became very interesting."

The hall went quiet again. Tense. Waiting for a fight. Only to be interrupted.

Another figure appeared at the top of the staircase.

This one moved differently.

Confident. Deliberate.

She stepped down slowly, black boots echoing softly against the marble steps. Her dark hair flowed over a leather jacket, and her sharp blue eyes scanned the room like she was already in control of it.

I frowned.

"…There's another one?"

Cameron leaned closer, laughing, "Looks like it is your lucky night."

Zebedee said, "Oh, this is definitely not part of the normal show."

The woman descended the staircase with a calm intensity, the golden light from the stained-glass window blazing behind her.

Unlike the first woman, she wasn't dramatic.

She was direct.

Purposeful.

Zebedee's smile faded slightly.

"Well," he murmured.

“That’s unexpected.”

Susan tilted her head.

“Do you know her?”

Zebedee adjusted his glasses slowly.

“She has a violent disposition.”

I glanced back at him with the facial expression of someone who had just eaten worms.

“That doesn’t sound reassuring.”

The woman reached the bottom of the stairs and walked straight toward the center of the room.

Straight toward me.

The first mysterious woman turned slightly, studying her arrival with narrowed eyes.

Claire whispered under her breath.

“Oh wow.”

I fretted.

“Why do I feel like I just walked into the middle of a competition I didn’t sign up for?”

The second woman stopped only a few feet away.

Her voice was cool and confident.

“Relax.”

She looked directly at me.

"You're not the prize."

She smiled slightly.

"You're the problem."

I stared at Zebedee.

"The problem?"

Zebedee didn't answer immediately. His expression had changed — the playful confidence was gone, replaced with something far more serious.

Cameron looked between them.

"OK," he said quietly.

I pointed toward the staircase, trying to hide my shakes.

Then back to Zebedee.

"Somehow *I'm* the problem?"

Zebedee sighed softly and adjusted his goggles.

Across the hall, the two women now stood several meters apart, both watching me with equal intensity, waiting for my answer. The crowd had fallen completely silent, sensing that something far more complicated than a simple "Girlfriend Factory" was unfolding.

Cameron leaned closer to Zebedee.

Zebedee hesitated.

"Ryan wasn't supposed to be here tonight."

I frowned.

Zebedee nodded slowly.

"This place… doesn't usually invite people."

I crossed my arms.

Zebedee looked directly at me.

"Maybe that is my fault."

Zebedee gave a small, uneasy smile.

I held my hand out firmly.

"No."

The single word cut through the silence like a blade.

"No to both."

The woman stopped.

For a moment, nothing moved. Magical sparkle charged the air.

The lights from the stained glass flickered across the marble floor, and the crowd seemed to hold its breath.

Cameron slowly leaned toward Zebedee.

"…He just rejected another …."

Zebedee watched me carefully, his expression thoughtful rather than surprised.

“Yes,” he said quietly.

I kept my hand raised.

“I didn’t come here for whatever this is.”

“Whatever happened to true love? Whatever happened to romance? I thought I was here tonight to meet my soul partner? My twin flame. The person I was born to be with until death.”

I glanced at the staircase, then at the two women watching me.

“I just wanted a normal night.”

Susan folded her arms, amused.

“Well,” she said to Claire, “that ship sailed about thirty minutes ago.”

Claire nodded.

“Yeah… we’re way past normal.”

The dark-haired woman at the base of the stairs studied me with intense curiosity.

Most men in the hall looked either nervous or eager.

I looked stubborn.

Defiant.

She took another step toward me.

I didn’t move.

Zebedee tilted his head slightly.

“Ryan,” he said calmly, “you may want to reconsider.”

I shook my head.

“No.”

Zebedee sighed.

“You misunderstand.”

I frowned.

“No, I think I understand perfectly…”

Zebedee raised one finger.

I blinked.

“…What?”

Zebedee nodded toward the glowing staircase behind her.

Across the room, the massive stained-glass window pulsed with a sudden flash of golden light.

The crowd murmured nervously.

Cameron whispered,

“OK… that doesn’t sound good.”

Zebedee looked at me with a mixture of sympathy and curiosity.

“Because,” he said quietly,

"There is one more."

The music suddenly surged back to life.

The DJs slammed the beat back into the room, and the crowd erupted again as the tension broke like a storm, releasing pressure.

Lights swept across the hall.

The disco ball scattered sparks of color across the thousands of people packed into the enormous ballroom.

I blinked in confusion.

Claire laughed and grabbed Zebedee's arm.

"What happened is you just became the most interesting person in the room."

Susan grinned at Steve.

"You rejected the witches."

I looked around at the cheering crowd.

"That was not my intention."

Zebedee clapped him on the shoulder.

"Nevertheless… congratulations."

I frowned.

"For what?"

Cameron gestured toward the growing circle forming around them on the dance floor.

"Oh, I don't know."

I looked down.

Everyone in their group had instinctively formed a circle, hands linked.

I groaned.

Zebedee smiled.

He nodded toward the staircase.

"The last one is coming, this one will be good."

I looked up.

At the top of the grand staircase, the stained-glass doors slowly began to open again.

And this time…

One more silhouette appeared. A familiar silhouette. One that could have been following me all night, and through my own ignorance, I have not noticed.

The crowd fell silent again.

From the glowing staircase, another woman appeared.

She moved with effortless confidence, her black dress flowing with each step. A streak of electric blue ran through her dark hair, catching the golden light as she descended. Her shiny black PVC dress, interspersed with deep black cotton, captured the light and drew eyes relentlessly.

I stared. I could not believe my eyes. I heard myself breaking my own rules.

"… OK." The words fell out of my mouth without conscious control. I had no control.

Cameron leaned closer.

"That one looks dangerous."

Susan smirked.

"They all look dangerous."

Claire tilted her head slightly, studying the newcomer.

"No," she said quietly. "That one knows exactly what she's doing."

The woman continued down the staircase, each step slow and deliberate. The entire hall watched as if the building itself had paused to see what would happen next.

Zebedee exhaled softly.

"Well."

I looked at him.

"Well, what?"

Zebedee adjusted his goggles.

“That confirms it.”

I frowned.

“Confirms what?”

Zebedee nodded toward the staircase.

The blue-haired woman reached the bottom of the stairs and stopped.

Her dark eyes locked onto me. A small smile on her lips.

Zebedee smiled slightly, looking for my answer.

I groaned.

Cameron slowly nodded and gestured toward the staircase, eager for my response.

I stared at Zebedee.

Zebedee nodded slowly.

“Yes?”

I rubbed my face in torture.

“I rejected two women…”

Cameron shrugged.

“Technically,” he said.

I groaned.

“That’s somehow worse.”

Across the hall, the women who had descended the staircase now stood spaced apart, watching me carefully. The crowd had shifted from cheering to whispering.

Susan leaned toward Claire.

“I think he broke the system.”

Claire nodded thoughtfully.

“Yeah… this doesn’t look like the usual program anymore.”

I turned back to Zebedee.

“Tell me exactly what happens. Is this my life partner? I am confused?”

Zebedee hesitated.

I crossed my arms.

Zebedee gestured subtly toward the staircase.

“Yes, life partner, she chooses you, do you choose her?”

I followed his gaze.

At the top of the staircase, the stained-glass doors were still open.

More shadows moved behind them.

I slowly exhaled.

Cameron shook his head.

"No?"

He looked at the staircase.

I blinked.

Zebedee adjusted his goggles.

I looked back toward the staircase.

Zebedee smiled gently.

"Oh no."

He gestured toward the enormous doors of the ballroom.

They had quietly closed.

"And now?" Zebedee said,

I suddenly started laughing.

The tension in the room cracked like glass.

"OK," he said, still smiling, holding my hand up.

"Yes."

The crowd froze.

Cameron blinked, surprised.

"…You changed your answer?"

I shrugged.

"I mean… I feel like …… I kind of like this is the one?"

Susan burst out laughing.

"Fair point."

Claire grinned.

"Honestly? That might be the smartest decision anyone's made tonight."

Across the hall, the women watching him exchanged angry, subtle glances.

The blue-streaked woman tilted her head with interest.

The first dark-cloaked woman raised one eyebrow.

Zebedee chuckled quietly.

"Ah, now the fun starts."

I looked at him.

"What?"

Zebedee tapped the side of his goggles.

I blinked.

Cameron crossed his arms.

Zebedee nodded approvingly.

The music shifted again, slower, heavier, dramatic.

At the top of the staircase, the glowing doors opened wider.

The silhouettes behind them began to move.

I squinted.

Zebedee smiled.

Zebedee gestured toward him.

The music swelled again, deeper now, almost theatrical.

I looked up at the staircase.

The golden doors at the top glowed like a sunrise behind stained glass.

The crowd pressed closer, hands raised, cheering as the lights swept across the hall.

Cameron leaned toward me.

"So… this is the part where we find out whether we accidentally volunteered you to be sacrificed to a secret society."

I laughed nervously.

Beside them, Susan squeezed my arm.

"Look."

The lights focused on the staircase.

The room quieted.

Even the DJ lowered the music.

Zebedee tipped his tall hat slightly, smiling as if he had seen this moment a thousand times.

The entire hall held its breath.

CHAPTER 26

Francis

The woman with the blue streak in her hair paused halfway down the staircase.

The lights shimmered across her black dress as she looked at my outstretched hand.

For a moment, the noise of the hall faded behind them.

She studied me carefully.

Then a slow smile appeared.

"You skipped several steps," she said calmly.

I blinked.

"...There are steps?"

She glanced over her shoulder toward the staircase.

"Technically."

"Well... I figured the direct approach might save everyone some time."

Her smile widened slightly.

I grinned.

Behind me, Cameron whispered loudly to Zebedee.

"I give him thirty seconds before he accidentally proposes marriage."

Zebedee stroked his chin thoughtfully.

"Oh, I think he's doing rather well."

The woman turned back to me.

Her blue-highlighted hair caught the light as she tilted her head.

"You asked me to dance."

I nodded.

"Yes."

She extended her hand slowly.

"Then don't just stand there."

My eyes widened slightly.

"Oh."

I took her hand.

The music shifted.

And the crowd around them erupted into cheers as they stepped onto the dance floor.

Francis placed her hand lightly into mine.

Her grip was confident.

The music softened as the lights above the dance floor shifted into a slow spiral of gold and blue.

I smiled.

She tilted her head slightly.

“My name is Francis, nice to meet you.”

I blinked.

Zebedee raised his glass toward us.

I sighed.

“My name is Ryan,” I said nervously.

Francis laughed quietly.

The music slowed into a smooth rhythm.

I gently placed one hand on her back.

She stepped closer.

“You do realize,” Francis said softly, “that everyone in this room is watching you right now.”

I glanced around.

The entire hall had formed a circle around the dance floor.

Susan looked delighted.

Claire whispered something excitedly.

I turned back to Francis.

“…No pressure then.”

Francis smiled.

"None at all."

The music rose.

And we began to dance.

CHAPTER 27

The Dance

The music softened into a slow, sweeping rhythm.

Francis and I moved together across the dance floor, the golden light of the chandeliers gliding across her dark dress as it flowed around them.

I looked slightly surprised.

“You’re really good at this.”

Francis raised an eyebrow.

“You sound shocked.”

“I was expecting to step on your feet at least twice by now.”

Francis smiled faintly.

“You still might.”

They turned gently with the music.

Around them, other couples joined the floor, but the circle of onlookers still kept a respectful distance, watching.

I lowered my voice.

“So… Francis.”

“Yes?”

"This place…"

He glanced toward the staircase, the glowing windows, the watching crowd.

"…is definitely not a normal nightclub."

Francis laughed quietly.

"No."

I leaned in slightly.

"So what *is* it?"

Francis held my gaze for a moment as they turned slowly beneath the chandelier.

Then she answered.

"It's where people come to see who they really are."

I blinked.

"That sounds… suspiciously philosophical for a dance club."

Francis smiled.

"You asked."

They spun again with the music.

Across the room, Zebedee watched them carefully, a small approving smile on his face.

The dance floor slowly filled with other couples.

But somehow Francis and I remained at the center of it all.

We moved smoothly across the polished floor, turning beneath the warm glow of the chandeliers. The music echoed through the vast hall like something older than the building itself.

I looked around at the swirling dancers.

Francis smiled.

I glanced down at our hands.

“I didn’t realize dancing counted as an exam.”

Francis stepped closer as we turned.

“It doesn’t.”

I raised an eyebrow.

“Then what does?”

Francis met my eyes.

“How you treat the person you’re dancing with.”

I paused for a moment as we moved together through the music.

Francis laughed softly.

Across the room, Cameron leaned against the railing, watching.

Back on the dance floor, I spun Francis gently beneath the chandelier.

The crowd around us clapped as she turned gracefully and returned to my arms.

Francis looked up at me, impressed.

"You really didn't know how to dance before tonight?"

I shrugged.

"I may have watched a few tutorial videos once."

Francis smiled.

"Well…"

She leaned slightly closer.

"You're learning very quickly."

CHAPTER 28

Bouncy Castle Party

Francis stopped mid-step. Her facial expression showed a curious question.

For a moment, the music continued around us while she simply stared at me.

"A… bouncy castle party?" she asked.

I nodded earnestly.

"Yes, let's go."

They turned slowly with the music as if the conversation were completely normal.

"I got invited earlier this week," she said. "Apparently, there are three castles, a foam machine, and unlimited pizza."

Francis blinked.

I shrugged.

"You're asking me… to leave this enormous mysterious ballroom… full of chandeliers and orchestras…"

"…for a giant inflatable castle, in the middle of the night?"

She smiled.

"Well, when you put it like that, it sounds even better."

Francis tried to keep a straight face.

She failed.

A laugh escaped before she could stop it.

Francis shook her head, still smiling.

"You're either completely ridiculous…"

I waited.

"…or you're the most honest person in this entire building."

I grinned.

"I'm aiming for both."

Francis studied me for another moment as the music swirled around us.

Then she leaned closer.

Francis smiled slowly.

"Well then…"

She squeezed my hand slightly.

CHAPTER 29

Leaving

Outside, the factory glowed against the night sky.

Warm golden light poured from its tall windows, reflecting across the dark water of the canal. Steam drifted lazily from the towering chimneys, and the stained-glass clock face shimmered like a watchful eye over the city.

Inside, the music still echoed faintly through the walls.

Couples danced.

Laughter drifted into the night air.

At the entrance, Zebedee stepped out onto the stone walkway and looked up at the enormous building.

He adjusted his goggles and smiled to himself.

"Another successful evening," he murmured.

Behind him, Cameron pushed open the door and stepped outside.

He looked up at the towering smokestacks.

"So… how many people leave here with dates?"

Zebedee chuckled.

"Not many."

Cameron frowned.

"…That seems like a bad success rate for a girlfriend factory."

Zebedee shook his head.

"You misunderstand."

He glanced back toward the glowing ballroom doors.

"This place doesn't make girlfriends."

Cameron raised an eyebrow.

"What does it make?"

Zebedee smiled.

"Stories."

CHAPTER 30

The After Party

The bouncy castle party was already in full swing.

Music drifted across the park from a portable speaker balanced on a picnic table. Strings of colored lights hung between the trees, swaying gently in the night breeze. People laughed, ran, and bounced inside the enormous inflatable castle that loomed like a glowing yellow fortress in the dark.

I stopped at the entrance and folded my arms.

I studied the structure like an engineer inspecting a questionable bridge.

"This," I said carefully, "feels significantly less structurally sound than the factory."

Francis followed my gaze upward.

The castle creaked.

"I'm still not convinced this is safer."

Behind them, Cameron burst out laughing.

"You two met in a secret ballroom with chandeliers and mysterious music… and the thing that worries you is a bouncy castle?"

Susan stepped beside him, smiling.

"I think it's adorable."

Nearby, Zebedee stood calmly talking with Claire, sipping a drink as if attending a midnight inflatable castle party was perfectly normal.

Francis turned back to me.

"So," she nodded toward the castle.

"Do we dance in there, too?"

I grinned.

"I think the official rule is you have to jump first."

Francis raised an eyebrow.

"And if I fall?"

I held out my hand.

"Then I'll catch you."

She looked at me for a moment, measuring the sincerity in my voice.

Then I placed her hand in mine.

"Alright," she said softly.

"Let's see how well you dance in zero gravity."

They stepped inside.

The floor sank beneath our feet and bounced us upward. I staggered slightly as the castle lurched.

Francis laughed, the kind of laugh that comes when gravity suddenly becomes optional.

I grabbed her waist to steady her.

The music outside faded into the background rhythm.

For a moment, it felt strangely familiar.

Like the ballroom.

Only now were the chandeliers replaced by colored plastic towers, and the dance floor squeaked.

But somehow the feeling was the same.

I looked at her.

“Still dancing?”

Francis smiled.

“Still dancing.”

And together we jumped.

CHAPTER 31

The Quiet Moment

The party slowly began to settle.

Music softened. Conversations drifted into quieter corners of the park.

Francis and I sat on the grass near the edge of the lights, watching the last few people bouncing inside the castle.

The night air had cooled.

For a while, neither of us spoke.

Finally, Francis said, “That was… not how I expected tonight to end.”

I nodded.

“Honestly, neither did I.”

She leaned back on her hands.

“We started in a ballroom that might not even exist.”

“And ended in a bouncy castle.”

I considered that.

“Technically a structural downgrade.”

Francis laughed.

Then her expression softened.

"But it felt real."

I looked at her.

"What did?"

"This," she said.

She gestured to the lights, the music, the friends scattered around the park.

"You."

I was quiet for a moment.

"You know," I said, "I spent a long time thinking dating was some complicated system."

Francis tilted her head.

"You would."

"I thought there were rules. Algorithms. Steps."

"And?"

I shrugged.

"I think it might just be this."

I gestured around them.

"Showing up."

Francis nodded slowly.

"That sounds about right."

They sat in comfortable silence again.

Then Francis asked,

“So… what happens after the after party?”

I smiled.

“I guess we find out.”

CHAPTER 32

How to Date

Later that night, the park had nearly emptied.

The lights were being taken down.

The bouncy castle deflated slowly with a long sigh, collapsing like a tired giant.

Francis and I walked along the path toward the exit.

"You know," Francis said, "if someone asked me how to date…"

I groaned.

"Oh no."

"…I'd probably say it starts with dancing in a mysterious ballroom."

I shook my head.

"That is absolutely not a replicable strategy."

"And ends with jumping in a bouncy castle."

"That part might be."

Francis stopped walking.

She turned to face me.

"But seriously."

I waited.

“I think the real trick,” she said, “is finding someone who’s willing to look a little ridiculous with you.”

I smiled.

“That seems like a very dangerous standard.”

“Why?”

“Because,” I said, “we just spent twenty minutes bouncing around like astronauts.”

Francis grinned.

“Exactly.”

I laughed.

“Fair point, more bouncing?”

We resumed bouncing.

And for once, neither of us felt like we needed a plan.

CHAPTER 33

The Kiss

Inside the bouncy castle, the world felt completely different. Cocooned. Silent.

The soft inflatable floor shifted gently beneath us. Laughter echoed around the colorful walls.

Francis and I had finally stopped trying to stand.

Instead, we sat together on the gently rising surface, still holding hands.

I looked around.

"I feel like we've entered a completely different universe."

Francis smiled.

"It's definitely less dramatic than the factory."

I leaned a little closer.

"So… I think we may have ..."

Francis tilted her head.

"Ballroom dancing in an inflatable castle?"

I nodded.

"It could become a trend."

Francis laughed softly.

“I doubt the ballroom crowd is ready for that level of chaos.”

Another bounce shifted the floor, and we both leaned slightly toward each other.

I smiled.

“Well…”

I squeezed her hand gently.

“…I’m glad you said yes.”

Francis looked at me for a moment.

“So am I.”

The castle floor shifted gently beneath us.

For a moment, everything else faded.

The laughter outside, the music from the speakers, it all seemed far away.

Francis and I leaned toward each other.

Our hands were still clasped between us.

Then we kissed.

It was soft at first, slightly awkward because the inflatable floor bounced unexpectedly beneath us.

Francis pulled back just enough to laugh.

“This might be the only kiss in history with built-in suspension.”

I smiled.

“I think it improves the experience.”

The castle bounced again, nudging us closer.

CHAPTER 34

Let's All Go to the Beach

I blinked.

"The beach?"

Francis smiled, the faint blue streak in her hair catching the streetlights from outside the inflatable castle.

"Yes."

I looked around the bouncy castle.

"...You realize we're currently inside an inflatable medieval fortress in the middle of a park."

Francis tilted her head.

"And?"

I grinned.

"Just checking the travel logistics."

Francis stepped closer and took my hand again.

"The sunrise is in about an hour."

Francis smiled.

"I plan ahead."

The park gates stood open beneath the streetlights.

Francis and I paused before leaving.

Behind them, the last of the lights flickered off.

The party was officially over.

Francis looked back one last time.

Outside the castle, Cameron noticed us heading for the exit.

"Wait… are they leaving?"

Susan looked surprised.

"Already?"

Zebedee simply nodded.

Claire frowned slightly.

Zebedee looked toward the sky, where the first faint hint of dawn was beginning to lighten the horizon.

"The best part of a story," I said calmly, "usually happens just before sunrise."

Francis stepped out.

I followed.

And together we headed toward the quiet road that led to the beach.

CHAPTER 35

Sunrise

She looked toward the sky.

“Now let’s go to the beach and watch the sunrise.”

An hour later, the sky turned gold.

Francis, I, and our friends ran across the sand together as the sun rose over the ocean.

Waves crashed against our feet while birds circled above the water.

The night was over.

But something new had begun.

I looked toward the horizon.

And for the first time in a long time…

Everything felt possible. Not the end of a story.

But at the beginning of whatever came next.

The truth was, getting a girlfriend wasn’t magic.

It was just talking to someone like they mattered.

Uncle Ryan looked down at the perfectly sleeping Mathew. The story had done its job.

In the main room, a noise was made. Someone moved, possibly a person with a streak of blue in her hair. Ryan smiled.

The End

If you like this book, please read the other titles by the same author via Amazon KDP.

Tanks on a Spaceship
https://www.amazon.com/dp/B0GRG6B496

Intergalactic Junkyard
https://www.amazon.com/dp/B0GSF9DML2

The Note Singer
https://www.amazon.com/dp/B0GX2YLXQY

Spaceship Salvage
https://www.amazon.com/dp/B0GZ35KF5J

Any review would be greatly appreciated.

www.ingramcontent.com/pod-product-compliance
Lightning Source LLC
LaVergne TN
LVHW010620100826
845148LV00014B/3044